Terror

SHIVERS

Terror

by Terry Deary

WATTS BOOKS
London · New York · Sydney

© Terry Deary 1995

Watts Books

96 Leonard Street

London EC2A 4RH

Franklin Watts

14 Mars Road

Lane Cove

NSW

UK ISBN: 0 7496 2183 4

10 9 8 7 6 5 4 3 2 1

Dewey Decimal Classification 001.9

Editor: Rosemary McCormick

Designer: Mike Davis, Ian Probert

Author: Terry Deary

Cover Artist: Mark Taylor

Line Illustrator: Terry Oakes

Printed in Great Britain by
The Guernsey Press Co. Ltd., Guernsey, Channel Islands

Contents

Introduction   7

1. "Let me out! Let me out!"   9

2. "Mind the coffin, sir."   21

3. "I don't believe in ghosts."   33

4. "We will torment you . . ."   47

5. "I order you, most evil spirit . . ."   59

6. "Six foot under now."   71

7. "Don't go on the moors."   83

The following titles are also available:

Mystery
Spooks
Disaster

Introduction

Don't be afraid of the dark. The dark never hurt anyone. It's what's out there in the dark that can be so frightening.

Find a safer way to shiver with excitement. Read about the terrors other people have faced in their lives. But put the lights on first. Lock out the cold night air and lock out the inky darkness. Check that there's nothing under the chair or up the chimney. Find a warm, cosy place to sit. Nothing can hurt you . . . well, hardly anything. You have nothing to fear *except* your fear.

So open this book, if you dare, and read about people who've faced death and horror, misery and pain, yet lived to tell the tale . . . well, *sometimes* lived.

These stories are all based upon reports that someone, somewhere, has sworn are true. The fact files may spill some light into the shadows that hide the truth. Or they may hide that truth darker and deeper than ever.

1. "Let me out! Let me out!"

Graveyards are quiet and gloomy places. If you're a nervous person then a graveyard is just the sort of place where you may fear to go after dark. But are you right to be afraid? There shouldn't be anything there that could harm you . . .

Suffolk, England – October 1911
"The graveyard is a peaceful place," the vicar said. "The dead are laid to rest. To rest in peace."

"So, you don't believe in ghosts?" Doctor Joseph said, raising a tired eyebrow.

The log fire crackled in the grate of the hearth, yet it felt cold in the room. The wind moaned through the trees in the garden. Dead, dry leaves rattled against the window like hail. The Reverend Palmer looked at the flames for a long time before he answered.

"Yes, Doctor Joseph, I believe in ghosts. Some poor tormented souls die. They leave some unfinished

9

business here on earth. They cannot make the journey to the afterlife until they solve the problem," the vicar said carefully. He was a young man with a face as pink and round as the cherubs in the vicarage paintings.

The old doctor leaned forward. "What sort of 'unfinished business', Vicar?"

The young man shrugged. "Perhaps some sin that has gone unpunished. Maybe that's why the ghost speaks to me. The ghost could be trying to tell me about it because I'm the vicar. That's why no one else hears his voice."

The doctor leaned back in his chair and pulled the rug around his knees. "That's not quite true, Vicar."

The young man blinked. "You've heard the voice?"

The old man shook his head quickly. Too quickly. Pain made him take a sharp breath. "I meant that the other vicars have heard the voice too."

The vicar's blink grew more rapid. He put his hands together as if he were praying and rubbed them together with a soft rasping sound. "You know I always thought it strange. This parish has had thirty vicars in the last fifty years. None of them seems to stay for long. If they've all been bothered by the voice then that would explain it. Did some of them come to you?"

"Yes," the doctor said. "I tried to give them tonics for their nerves but at last it grew too much for them. They left."

The vicar jumped to his feet. The firelight reflected in his glowing eyes. "But that's not the answer," he groaned. "If there is some tormented soul out there in

10

the graveyard, he should be laid to rest. His story should be looked into. Perhaps it's a simple matter of a few prayers or an exorcism."

The doctor's face grew harder. "Don't think the other vicars didn't try. No one managed to discover the ghost's story. Every time they walked through the graveyard the ghost cried out to them, 'Let me out! Let me out!' but it never says anything else."

The young man was pacing up and down in front of the fire now. "If they only tried to talk to it! I must. For the sake of the poor, suffering soul. If you'll excuse me, I'll go right now."

"You don't want that tonic for your nerves, then?" the old doctor asked.

"No. No thank you. My nerves aren't the problem – I don't have a problem. It's some unfortunate spirit in the graveyard that has the problem. I must try to help," he said as he picked up his coat from the back of the chair and buttoned it all the way up to his chubby pink throat. "Don't get up, Doctor. I can see myself out, thanks," he added before picking up his black felt hat and hurrying to the door.

The autumn wind tried to snatch the hat from his head as he leaned into the flurries of its cold breath, which carried showers of dead leaves. They flew into his face like pale golden bats. When he reached the corner of the road he turned towards the church and left the last gas street lamp behind him.

The vicar slowed as he reached the gate to the churchyard. He straightened up, pulled his hat off and clutched it to his chest. Lifting the latch on the gate, he stepped into the graveyard. Marble gravestones

11

glowed faintly in the light that spilled from the distant road.

The tall churchyard wall sheltered the graves and there was an eerie calm in here while the tall trees groaned overhead. And tonight, when the young man wanted to talk to the troubled spirit, the ghost was silent. "Are you there?" he called. His voice echoed back from the grim, grey church. "I want to help you!" But no one and nothing answered.

The vicar pulled his hat back on and hurried out of the gate. He slithered over the damp leaves on the path and hurried back to the vicarage. The porch light was as welcome as a lighthouse to a lost sailor. In the living-room the fire was still glowing. With a poker, he stirred it back into life and held his pale hands up to the flames.

There was a noise behind him. A soft scratching like a cat's claw on a gravestone. Someone was trying to get in through the window; the window that overlooked the churchyard. The vicar stepped across to it and pulled the curtain back.

He gave a gasping cry as shocked as a man falling into an icy sea. The face that looked back at him was moon-white and glowing. Its eyes were wide with terror and the claw-hands seemed to be tearing at the air in front of it. The hands weren't touching the glass yet the vicar could hear that scratch-scratch-scratch. The phantom's colourless lips seemed to be saying something. There was no sound, but the young vicar, more rigid than an icicle, knew what it was saying. "Let me out! Let me out!"

The young man clutched a hand to his shuddering

heart, nodded at the vision and cried, "I'll come to you, my friend. Wait!" before he rushed to the door and out into the damp grass.

No one stood outside the living-room window. But from across the garden wall the familiar voice wailed, "Let me out! Let me out!" The young man's fingers tore at the wall until they bled. He scrambled at any small foothold or fingerhold and raised his head over the wall.

The graveyard was dark as ever but the voice echoed around it, "Let me out! Let me out!"

"What is it? What's wrong? Tell me . . . tell me who you are! I can help you!"

But the only reply was thin as the east wind, "Let me out, let me out!"

At last the vicar's grip loosened on the top of the wall and he slipped back into the vicarage garden. He rested a cheek against the cool wall, closed his eyes and murmured a prayer. Then he felt a tickle at his wrist and realised blood from his torn hand was running down his arm.

He trudged across the grass towards the warmth of the house and decided he'd need to visit the doctor again tomorrow.

After a restless night's sleep he woke to a hammering on the door. The village postman handed him some letters and said cheerfully, "Morning, Reverend. I've a message from the doctor. He says can you call round to see him this morning?"

"Of course."

"At his house – not the surgery. He'll not be holding many more surgeries," the postman said with a shake of his head. "He's a sick man is Doctor Joseph . . . come to think of it, you don't look too grand yourself."

"Ah . . . no. Bad night's sleep."

"Bad night's sleep? You look like you've seen a ghost! Good day, Reverend." With that the man plodded back down the drive.

The vicar shaved quickly, the razor clumsy in his torn hand. He dressed and set off for the doctor's house.

Doctor Joseph was sitting by the fire. His face was dust grey with deep charcoal lines. "Are you all right?" the vicar asked. His pink face creased with worry as he remembered the postman's words. He'd been too worried about his own problems last night to notice the frailness of the old doctor.

The doctor looked at him with tired, old eyes. "No, Vicar. I am dying. I know what is wrong with me. I know there is no cure. That's the trouble with being a doctor. You can't lie to yourself."

"I'm sorry," his visitor said helplessly. "So sorry. If there's anything I can do . . ."

"There is," Doctor Joseph said quickly. "I don't want to end up like that ghost in your churchyard. I don't want to die with some – what did you call it? – unfinished business. I want to tell you a story. Please take a seat."

The old man leaned back and closed his eyes. He began speaking in a weary voice. "My story concerns a man called Bartholomew Pennington. He lived in this village fifty years ago . . . and he was probably the most hated man in the county. He was rich as a king

14

but mean, so mean. He couldn't bring himself to share anything. For all his money he refused to pay his bills. The tradesmen hated him."

"Why didn't they just stop supplying him?" the vicar asked quietly.

The doctor half-opened his eyes and looked across at him. "Because Pennington had a beautiful and charming wife, and they liked her a lot – God knows why she married him. Of course Pennington himself believed she'd married him for his money. Remember he didn't like sharing. He believed he was sharing his wife with another man. The fool came up with a crazy scheme to try to prove it."

"He spied on his wife?" the vicar asked.

The doctor gave a faint smile. "No. This was the *really* crazy idea. He called in the village doctor and told him his secret fears. 'I believe my wife has been seeing another man,' he said. 'She swears she loves me, but I don't believe her. I want her to prove it. I want her to see me dead, then watch how she behaves. Will she cry over my coffin – or will she laugh? I want to know.' The young doctor asked how he could do that and Pennington told him his wild idea. He wanted the doctor to give him a drug. A drug that would make him appear dead."

"No doctor would do such a thing, surely," the vicar gasped.

The doctor's face reddened. "This doctor agreed. Pennington wanted to wake up in the coffin and see his wife's reaction. He said, 'On no account must you let the coffin be sealed, of course.' The young doctor gave him the drug – but he gave him a huge amount of the sleeping drug, then told the beautiful Mrs Pennington that her husband had died. The local carpenter came and measured the man for his coffin – Pennington owed the man money so the carpenter was whistling as they put the body in. He was laughing as he screwed the lid down tight."

The vicar's pink face was pale now. "But Pennington was asleep, not dead, surely. He'd wake up in the coffin!"

The doctor nodded. "One of the coffin carriers swore he heard a scratching at the lid. The carpenter laughed and said it was impossible. Then they buried the coffin."

The young vicar looked as if he would be sick. "Buried alive? That's murder!"

"Buried alive," the old doctor nodded. "Murder."

"But why?" his visitor cried.

"You'll understand if I tell you that the young doctor married the beautiful – rich and beautiful – Mrs Pennington."

"That is evil," the vicar said and his soft face turned hard. Then his jaw began to drop and his mouth opened into a small 'O'. "The ghost in the churchyard . . . it cries 'Let me out!' Is that the ghost of Pennington? No wonder it can't rest. It's remembering the terror of waking up inside its own coffin. It won't rest until the murderers are brought to justice."

The old doctor nodded. "The doctor and Mrs Pennington were never happy with the dead man's money. She died after they'd been married just a few years."

"And the young doctor? What happened to him? You have to tell me. I must report him to the police. What is his name?"

"Leave it three weeks. Four at the most. Go to the police then. Tell the world. It won't matter then."

"Why not?" the young man asked.

The doctor opened his eyes wider now and looked at the vicar. "Because by then I will be dead." The vicar met his gaze with a look of horror. "That's right, Reverend. I was that young doctor. Now I want the murder off my mind before I die."

The vicar rose to his feet. He was numb. "You can't ask me to forgive you . . . all I can do is pray for you."

The doctor struggled painfully to sit upright. "No! There is one other thing you can do for me. Don't let me be buried in the village churchyard. Bury me in a ditch or bury me at sea. Bury me anywhere but don't bury me close to . . . him. Over the last fifty years the vicars have all heard his cries to be let out – but there's one other person who's heard him every single night. His murderer. Me. Every night. 'Let me out! Let me out!' Night after night. Please, Reverend, let my death be an end to it."

The young man picked up his hat and walked out of the door. "Please!" the doctor cried after him. "Please!"

It didn't take four weeks or even three. Within a few hours of his confession Doctor Joseph died.

That night the Reverend Palmer stood at the gateway to the churchyard. The wind had dropped. A light mist gathered in the tops of the trees. Drops of

17

water fell onto the granite gravestones. There was no other sound. There was no voice.

When he returned to the vicarage there was no face at the window. He looked across the darkened garden. "Well, Mr Pennington, it seems you can rest at last."

The cries of "Let me out!" were never heard again.

Buried alive — FACT FILE

This story was collected by a "ghost-hunter" who travelled the country talking to people who claimed to have had supernatural experiences.

It is terrible, but true, that people have been declared dead when they in fact were alive. However, the ones who have woken-up in their coffins have not always come back as ghosts to tell their story. Some interesting cases include . . .

1. Camerino University, Italy – 1950
Camerino University held classes in the study of the supernatural. At one of these classes the professor brought a spirit 'medium' to the class – a medium is someone who can go into a trance and pass on messages from the dead. At the first session the medium had a message from a woman called Rosa Manichelli. Rosa said she had gone into a coma in 1939 and been buried. She woke too late and found herself in her coffin. The spirit voice described the date and place exactly. The students investigated and

found that a woman of that name had been buried where the medium-spirit said. They gained permission to dig up the coffin. When the lid was opened the skeleton had its knees bent as if trying to force open the lid. There were scratches on the inside of the lid. It seems the medium was right about Rosa's fate. No one but Rosa – or her ghost – could possibly have known about her waking in the coffin.

2. Germany – 1852

A young woman fell ill with typhoid fever, died and was buried quickly so the disease would not have a chance to spread to the living. She was buried so quickly that her brother, who'd been away on business, missed her funeral. He arrived at the graveyard just as the gravediggers were filling the grave. The tearful brother insisted that they open the coffin so he could have one last look at his sister. After a long argument they finally unearthed the coffin and allowed him his wish. That was when they discovered she was breathing. The 'corpse' sat up in the coffin and her overjoyed brother helped her out. It was said she lived for many more years and raised a large family.

3. Manchester, England – 1758

John Beswick fell ill and the doctor said he was dead. After he had been placed in his coffin, his sister Hannah went to look at him one last time . . . and found he was still breathing. John was revived and lived another ten years. But Hannah was so shocked by the experience that she said she never wanted to be buried . . . ever. She left instructions that she was to be mummified and her remains kept above ground. The instructions were carried out, although a hundred years later Hannah was eventually buried. However, her spirit was never able to rest in peace. It continued to haunt her old house for another eighty years or so.

4. London, England – 1750
William Duell was hanged for a crime and his body was taken to a laboratory for surgeons to experiment with. As they laid him on the table they noticed that Duell was breathing. Instead of practising surgery on him, they practised the skills of reviving. They succeeded. In a while, he was sitting up drinking warm wine. He was sent back to prison where he said hanging hadn't been painful, it had only sent him into a peaceful and beautiful dream. The authorities decided it was unfair to hang him again, so they had him transported as a slave.

5. USA – 19th Century
So many people feared being buried alive that an American inventor came up with a device that could save you in such circumstances. Your coffin was fitted with an air tube, a periscope and a bell-pull so you could signal to people above that you were alive and kicking. There are no records, however, of anyone escaping live burial using one of these contraptions.

2. "Mind the coffin, sir!"

Some people believe that you can surround yourself with good luck by collecting charms. Some believe that certain actions bring you bad luck – walking under a ladder, for example. And some people also believe that certain objects carry their own bad luck with them. The objects are said to be "cursed" ...

London, England – 1972

The man kicked the coffin.

"I've just kicked the most expensive thing in the world," he said.

One of the two men who sat beside him laughed. "It wouldn't be so funny if the mummy lifted the coffin lid, reached out its hand and grabbed your leg!"

It was cool and dimly lit in the cargo hold of the aircraft. The crew were bored. Ian Liddell gave the coffin a second gentle kick and pulled out a pack of cards from his jacket pocket. "Anyone fancy a game?"

he asked.

"We haven't got a card table," Jim Watson said. "Or hadn't you noticed?"

"What's this?" Ian asked and tapped the coffin again with his foot.

"It's a coffin," Jim shrugged.

"It has a flat top. We can play cards on that!"

"You can't do that!" Brian Goodwin cried. "There's a body in there."

Ian sighed. "He's been dead three thousand years. They've dug him up and now they're flying him over to England to stick him in a museum. If the old mummy's going to get upset then he'll take it out on the people who unearthed him."

"Oh, but he already has," Brian said. He was the youngest of the crew on duty in the cargo hold. His wide eyes were blinking rapidly. "Haven't you heard about the curse?"

"I've heard lots of stories about the Mummy's curse," Ian Liddell said, shuffling the cards idly. "In fact, the curse was known about before they even found Tutankhamun here. There was a famous fortune teller called Count Louis Hamon. Have you heard about him?"

The other two shook their heads and Ian went on. "Hamon had a lot of mystic powers and one of them was the ability to heal sick people when doctors had failed. He always charged a lot of money, of course, so only the rich could afford his help. Some time back in the 1890s he went across to Egypt and healed a rich sheikh. Not only did the sheikh pay him well . . . he also insisted on giving Hamon a gift. The hand of a

22

mummy."

"Gruesome," young Brian shuddered.

"It was. But the sheikh was a powerful man. You can't very well turn down a gift because he would be very offended. Hamon's wife hated the shrivelled thing even more than he did. Especially when she heard the story attached to it."

"A curse?" Jim Watson guessed

"No. Just a dreadful tale. It seems the hand belonged to a rich princess who quarrelled with her father." Ian Liddell turned over a card. It showed a king. In his hand was a sword. The man gave a slight smile. "The cruel king had the princess murdered and then – as an extra punishment – he had her hand cut off." The face of the king on the card looked suitably cruel.

Brian blinked again. "How is that an extra punishment? If she was dead then I'm sure she wouldn't mind her hand being cut off."

"Ah, but you're wrong!" Ian said and leaned forward. "The Egyptians believed that without a complete body you couldn't get into their heaven. She would spend the rest of time wandering the world just looking for her hand."

"So what did Hamon do with it?" Jim Watson asked.

"He tried to give it away to a museum – but no one wanted it. His wife wouldn't have it on show in their house so he had to lock it away in a safe. And there it stayed until one evening the countess opened the safe and screamed. The hand seemed softer and fresher than it had been before. It was almost alive."

23

Ian Liddell's hand riffled through the cards as he went on, "The countess insisted that Hamon should destroy it. He agreed that they should cremate it in their fireplace. Give it a decent funeral. And, of all nights, they chose 31 October – Halloween."

"Her ghost came back?" Brian said.

"And how!" Ian agreed. "As they laid the hand in the fireplace and began to read a passage from the Egyptian *Book of the Dead* to speed it on its way to the afterlife, the princess returned. There was a blast like thunder that rocked the house and sent it into darkness. The door flew open and a freezing wind blew in. Hamon and the countess threw themselves to the floor. As they looked up they saw a figure enter the room. It was a woman and she was dressed in long robes . . . robes of the type an Egyptian princess might have worn. But, most frightening of all was her arm. It ended in a stump where her hand should have been."

Jim Watson laughed. "How could they see all this if it was dark?"

Young Brian was blinking at machine-gun speed now. "Ghosts sort of glow, don't they?"

Jim Watson leaned back from the coffin and yawned. "Only if you believe in ghosts," he said.

"They'd lit the fire," Ian cut in. "They'd lit it to burn the hand. Anyway the princess figure moved towards the fireplace and reached out. Suddenly she vanished. When the Hamons looked, the mummified hand had disappeared. They never saw it again."

"Deal the cards, Ian," Jim said. "This has got nothing to do with the curse of Tutankhamun. The feller in the coffin."

"Ah, but that's where you're wrong!" Ian replied as he dealt the cards onto the coffin lid. "Count Hamon was a friend of Lord Caernarvon. And Lord Caernarvon was just about to set out for Egypt on an expedition to dig up a mummy. His partner had found a doorway into a cave. And over the doorway was a threat: 'Death to him who disturbs the pharaoh's sleep.' Lord Caernarvon was about to set out to break through that doorway. Hamon saw his experience with the mummy's hand as a sign – warning that his friend should not disturb the dead. He sent an urgent message to Caernarvon. It said, 'Do not enter the tomb. Disobey at your peril. Ignore this and you will suffer from sickness. You will not recover. You will die in Egypt.'"

"And he did!" Brian cut in eagerly. "The Egyptian museum manager told me the story last night while the staff were loading these crates. Doctor Mehrez didn't believe the curse. He said he'd had more to do with the tombs and the mummies than anyone else and he was still alive."

"Yeah, but what did Doctor Mehrez say about the ones who died," Ian asked.

Brian screwed up his face and tried to remember. "Let's see. It started with Lord Caernarvon, didn't it? He was bitten by a mosquito on the cheek. The infection killed him just two months after they'd broken into Tutankhamun's tomb."

"That was just bad luck," Jim Watson laughed. "Nothing sinister about that."

"But there were stories about his death, weren't

there? At the moment he died his dog howled – three thousand miles away in England – and it dropped down dead too. Then all the lights went out in Cairo. And after they'd unwrapped the body of Tutankhamun they found a mark on the mummy's cheek – on exactly the spot where Lord Caernarvon had been bitten!"

"Poppycock," Jim sighed.

"That's what Doctor Mehrez said," Brian agreed. "But there were so many deaths. Lord Caernarvon's best friend rushed to Egypt for the funeral and dropped down dead," Brian remembered.

"An old man, probably. The strain of the journey, the heat of Egypt. It could have killed anyone," Jim pointed out.

"I suppose so. Most of the people who died were old – the American archaeologist who helped Lord Caernarvon – Arthur Mace – he died not long after his lordship. Then Lord Caernarvon's personal secretary dropped dead . . . oh, and they sent an expert out from Britain to x-ray the mummy. He died as soon as he returned to Britain," Brian went on. He closed his eyes and concentrated. "After seven years only two of the original expedition were alive."

"Old men," Jim repeated. "Didn't the last survivor go on television a couple of years ago and rubbish the story of a curse?"

"Oh, yes," Brian said and his voice trembled with the beat of the aircraft engines. "But as he left the television studio his taxi crashed. He was thrown out and a lorry missed his head by inches!"

"Hah!" Jim snorted. "If there'd been a real curse

porters forget to mention the people
r from the curse. Doctor Derry gave
medical examination and came as
my as anyone. He lived ... to the age

rning to Lord Caernarvon is well
e are no witnesses to the story about
h the missing hand. Only Hamon and
itnesses to this event and they could
ken – or lying.

rn scientists have come up with
r the unhealthiness of Tutankhamun's
ve that Ancient Egyptian germs could
ed in the underground chamber. When
h 1922 the germs were still around to
eologists who visited the tomb. One
that the rocks around the tomb are
a the deadly element uranium; visitors
ed radiation poisoning. It is true that
ad found uranium rocks in their gold

curse:
tor Mehrez was the manager of the
the job had been held by Mohammed
m had been very much against moving
treasures to France in 1966. He
the mummy in Egypt. But he lost the
meeting. Ibrahim left the meeting and
path of a taxi. He died instantly.

then it would have flattened him."

"I suppose so," Brian muttered.

"And Doctor Mehrez has rubbished the curse. I'd put my money on him being right," Ian said. "So let's forget all about curses. Deal the cards."

Jim Watson chose a card and turned it over. "Ace of spades," Ian chuckled. "The death card. There's a bad omen for you!"

"Just as well I'm not one of those doddering old archaeologists then, isn't it?" Jim smiled.

Brian Goodwin didn't laugh. He was still feeling uneasy when the plane taxied to a standstill two hours later. He handed over the documents for the officer to check. "Who signed this in Cairo?" the man asked squinting at the signature.

"Ah, that's Doctor Mehrez," Brian explained. "The manager of the Cairo museum."

"He'll not be signing any more of these," the officer said. "Just had a radio report through from Cairo. Seems this Mehrez waved you off then dropped dead from a heart attack."

Brian Goodwin felt a strange tightening in his own chest as if some clammy hand had wrapped itself around his heart and squeezed it. "I was just talking to him a few hours ago," he said faintly.

"You feeling all right?" the officer asked him. "You look as if it's given you quite a turn."

Brian struggled to find his voice. "All right? Yes. All right. Just sit down a moment." He sank down onto the wooden chest behind him.

"Not on the coffin, sir, if you don't mind," the officer said gently.

In the following four years Brian Goodwin suffered two heart attacks. "It's the curse," he told his wife as he lay in hospital recovering from the second one.

"I know. You've told me," she said and chewed her lip with worry. "But you don't want to believe in it. It will only make you worse. You have to believe you'll get better. That's what the doctor says."

He lay back on the crisp white hospital pillows and closed his eyes. "It wasn't just poor Doctor Mehrez. There was the pilot of our plane – the one that brought Tutankhamun back from Egypt – he died, didn't he? Just two years after that flight. He was only forty-five."

"Yes," his wife admitted. "And the co-pilot died two years later. He was only forty?"

"Yes."

"And all they did was fly the plane. But me? Me . . . I played cards on the mummy's coffin. This is my punishment. Look at Jim Watson – his house burned to the ground, didn't it?"

"Yes."

"Only Ian Liddell seems to have escaped the curse," the sick man sighed.

This time his wife didn't answer. There was something about her silence that made him open his eyes and look at her. She was looking down at a paper handkerchief in her hands and tearing it to shreds. "What's wrong? What's happened to Ian?" he said sharply.

"Nothing. Well . . . nothing very serious. He was on a ladder doing some work when the ladder collapsed

28

2. *When Carter and Caernarvon had broken into Tutankhamun's tomb they stepped out into a sandstorm. As the storm cleared a hawk was seen hovering in the sky to the west . . . the direction of the Egyptians' 'Land of the Dead'. The bird seemed to be watching the archaeologists. The hawk was one of the symbols of the Egyptian royal family.*

3. *There are many other stories of mummies' curses. One mummified priestess was supposed to have been moved to an English museum. Douglas Murray found her in 1910. Soon after, he had a hunting accident in which his gun exploded. He had to have an arm amputated. His two expedition friends died and so did the servants who went on his archaeological trip. He gave the mummy to a woman friend – her mother died soon after, her fiancé left her and she fell ill. Murray offered it to a London museum where a photographer took pictures of the mummy – then dropped dead. A wagon-driver was crushed when the mummy's stone case fell off the wagon and pinned him against a wall. A museum caretaker also died.*

4. *On a visit to Egypt in 1936 Sir Alexander Seton saw the unwrapped remains of a mummy. His wife, Zeyla, wanted a souvenir so she stole a bone from the skeleton. From that time onward Sir Alexander and Zeyla seemed cursed. Ghostly figures appeared in the house, valuable ornaments were shattered when they fell to the floor in empty rooms. People who held the bone became ill. Finally Sir Alexander decided to*

have the bone 'exorcised' by his uncle, a monk. The bone was burned and the noises ended – but Sir Alexander's marriage to Zeyla was wrecked and he died an unhappy man . . . blaming the mummy's bone.

then it would have flattened him."

"I suppose so," Brian muttered.

"And Doctor Mehrez has rubbished the curse. I'd put my money on him being right," Ian said. "So let's forget all about curses. Deal the cards."

Jim Watson chose a card and turned it over. "Ace of spades," Ian chuckled. "The death card. There's a bad omen for you!"

"Just as well I'm not one of those doddering old archaeologists then, isn't it?" Jim smiled.

Brian Goodwin didn't laugh. He was still feeling uneasy when the plane taxied to a standstill two hours later. He handed over the documents for the officer to check. "Who signed this in Cairo?" the man asked squinting at the signature.

"Ah, that's Doctor Mehrez," Brian explained. "The manager of the Cairo museum."

"He'll not be signing any more of these," the officer said. "Just had a radio report through from Cairo. Seems this Mehrez waved you off then dropped dead from a heart attack."

Brian Goodwin felt a strange tightening in his own chest as if some clammy hand had wrapped itself around his heart and squeezed it. "I was just talking to him a few hours ago," he said faintly.

"You feeling all right?" the officer asked him. "You look as if it's given you quite a turn."

Brian struggled to find his voice. "All right? Yes. All right. Just sit down a moment." He sank down onto the wooden chest behind him.

"Not on the coffin, sir, if you don't mind," the officer said gently.

In the following four years Brian Goodwin suffered two heart attacks. "It's the curse," he told his wife as he lay in hospital recovering from the second one.

"I know. You've told me," she said and chewed her lip with worry. "But you don't want to believe in it. It will only make you worse. You have to believe you'll get better. That's what the doctor says."

He lay back on the crisp white hospital pillows and closed his eyes. "It wasn't just poor Doctor Mehrez. There was the pilot of our plane – the one that brought Tutankhamun back from Egypt – he died, didn't he? Just two years after that flight. He was only forty-five."

"Yes," his wife admitted. "And the co-pilot died two years later. He was only forty?"

"Yes."

"And all they did was fly the plane. But me? Me . . . I played cards on the mummy's coffin. This is my punishment. Look at Jim Watson – his house burned to the ground, didn't it?"

"Yes."

"Only Ian Liddell seems to have escaped the curse," the sick man sighed.

This time his wife didn't answer. There was something about her silence that made him open his eyes and look at her. She was looking down at a paper handkerchief in her hands and tearing it to shreds. "What's wrong? What's happened to Ian?" he said sharply.

"Nothing. Well . . . nothing very serious. He was on a ladder doing some work when the ladder collapsed

28

for some reason. Shattered his leg."

Brian looked up at the bright light over his head without blinking. "It was his right leg, wasn't it?"

"How did you know?"

He looked at his wife with just a hint of fear in his wide eyes. "That was the leg he used to kick the mummy's coffin," he said simply.

The Mummy's curse — FACT FILE

The curse of Tutankhamun's mummy has fascinated people since it first arose in the 1920s. Many of these reports have been inaccurate. Look at the facts below and make up your own mind . . .

The case against a curse:
1. The number of deaths connected to the Tutankhamun mummy is high but not so high that it proves a curse was at work. Lord Caernarvon's main archaeologist was an American called Howard Carter. Surely he should have died first? Carter, however, died of natural causes seventeen years after the excavation.

2. People who claimed a curse was at work took almost any death loosely linked to the mummy as evidence. The father of Carter's secretary died and was linked to the curse even though he had never been near the tomb or the mummy.

29

3. The curse supporters forget to mention the people who didn't suffer from the curse. Doctor Derry gave Tutankhamun a medical examination and came as close to the mummy as anyone. He lived . . . to the age of eighty-eight.

4. Hamon's warning to Lord Caernarvon is well known. But there are no witnesses to the story about the princess with the missing hand. Only Hamon and his wife were witnesses to this event and they could have been mistaken – or lying.

5. Some modern scientists have come up with explanations for the unhealthiness of Tutankhamun's tomb. They believe that Ancient Egyptian germs could have been trapped in the underground chamber. When it was opened in 1922 the germs were still around to infect the archaeologists who visited the tomb. One wild theory is that the rocks around the tomb are radioactive with the deadly element uranium; visitors may have suffered radiation poisoning. It is true that the Egyptians had found uranium rocks in their gold mines.

The case for a curse:
1. Before Doctor Mehrez was the manager of the Cairo museum the job had been held by Mohammed Ibrahim. Ibrahim had been very much against moving Tutankhamun's treasures to France in 1966. He fought to keep the mummy in Egypt. But he lost the fight in a final meeting. Ibrahim left the meeting and walked into the path of a taxi. He died instantly.

2. When Carter and Caernarvon had broken into Tutankhamun's tomb they stepped out into a sandstorm. As the storm cleared a hawk was seen hovering in the sky to the west . . . the direction of the Egyptians' 'Land of the Dead'. The bird seemed to be watching the archaeologists. The hawk was one of the symbols of the Egyptian royal family.

3. There are many other stories of mummies' curses. One mummified priestess was supposed to have been moved to an English museum. Douglas Murray found her in 1910. Soon after, he had a hunting accident in which his gun exploded. He had to have an arm amputated. His two expedition friends died and so did the servants who went on his archaeological trip. He gave the mummy to a woman friend – her mother died soon after, her fiancé left her and she fell ill. Murray offered it to a London museum where a photographer took pictures of the mummy – then dropped dead. A wagon-driver was crushed when the mummy's stone case fell off the wagon and pinned him against a wall. A museum caretaker also died.

4. On a visit to Egypt in 1936 Sir Alexander Seton saw the unwrapped remains of a mummy. His wife, Zeyla, wanted a souvenir so she stole a bone from the skeleton. From that time onward Sir Alexander and Zeyla seemed cursed. Ghostly figures appeared in the house, valuable ornaments were shattered when they fell to the floor in empty rooms. People who held the bone became ill. Finally Sir Alexander decided to

have the bone 'exorcised' by his uncle, a monk. The bone was burned and the noises ended – but Sir Alexander's marriage to Zeyla was wrecked and he died an unhappy man . . . blaming the mummy's bone.

3. "I don't believe in ghosts."

Some of the most frightening things in the world exist inside your own mind. If you have committed a crime then your own sense of guilt may torment you and drive you mad with fear. Is that what happened to Edwin Rutt, Captain of the SS Pierrot? Or is there a more sinister explanation . . .

London, England – 1885

"I don't believe in ghosts," the little man said. His clothes were scarecrow-tattered and his face as dirty-grey as the pavement outside the police station.

Police Sergeant Button's wide red face looked over the counter. The scruffy man didn't look mad, but you never could tell. In fact he looked quite intelligent, for a down-and-out. "No," he said. Then he added, "Sir."

"Someone is trying to murder me . . . and it isn't a ghost."

"No, sir."

33

"So I should be safe inside a police cell."

Sergeant Button frowned. "No, sir."

"No?"

"No, sir, I can't lock you up. Against the rules, see?"

The little man sighed. "You'd rather find me dead in some alley tomorrow morning than alive in your cell?"

The policeman scratched his chin and thought. Thinking was hard for Sergeant Button so he took a long time. Finally he said, "Ah."

"Exactly!" the man cried. "Just listen to my story, that's all I ask."

Sergeant Button sighed. "We have an interview room, sir, where we question suspects. We could go in there."

"Fine," the visitor snapped.

The policeman arranged for a young constable to take his place on the desk then plodded down the chilly corridor to a small room. He turned up the gas lamp, sat at a table and pulled out a notebook and pencil.

"Can we lock the door?" the visitor said. The man's eyes were red-rimmed as if he hadn't slept for days.

Sergeant Button shrugged before lumbering across to the door and selecting a key from a huge bunch on his belt, which he used to lock the door. The little man's shoulders dropped with relief. "Thanks," he said.

The policeman licked the end of his pencil, "Now, sir, can I have your name."

"Edwin Rutt. Captain Rutt."

"Army?" the policeman asked. The man didn't look like an army captain.

"Ship's captain. I was captain of the *Pierrot* till it sank last July. Capsized just north of the Azores."

The policeman tried a friendly smile, showing his smoke-stained teeth. "I thought a captain was supposed to go down with his ship?" he asked.

"Only if he's an idiot. And I am not an idiot, Sergeant."

"No, sir."

"Anyway only four of us survived. Me, the mate Josh Dudley, seaman Will Hoon . . . and the cabin-boy, Dick Tomlin. We managed to get into a dinghy with a little water but no food. Have you ever been hungry, Sergeant? I mean really hungry?"

The policeman was round as a barrel and two chins rolled over the collar of his dark blue uniform. "Oh, yes," he said.

"No. I mean really hungry . . . so hungry that you look at a man and you don't see a human being . . . you see a plate of food!"

The captain's eyes were wild and Sergeant Button began to wonder if the man was maybe mad after all. And what was he doing letting himself be locked in a room with him? He ran a finger nervously between his collar and his fat neck. "Er, no, sir, can't say I've ever had cannibal tendencies."

The sailor shook his head, "No. Not cannibal. Survival. That's what it's about. That's what we talked about those three weeks adrift in a life raft. We agreed that one man might die so three men could live, and that wasn't so terribly evil."

"It's against the law, sir," the sergeant said stiffly.

"Hah! You wouldn't arrest a shark for eating a man, would you?"

"No, but . . ."

"So why arrest a man?" the little man asked and his eyes were wilder now. "The only one who disagreed was young Dick Tomlin," he went on, softly now. "He said he wouldn't eat one of us, so . . ."

The sergeant's chins dropped. "You didn't?"

Captain Rutt nodded. "I killed him while he slept. He didn't suffer. But that's history now," he murmured.

"No, sir. You are confessing to a crime and you must be punished. I'll have to arrest you . . ."

"You can't!" the captain snapped and jumped to his feet. "A man can't be tried twice for the same crime." He paced the stone floor of the small room and explained impatiently, "We were rescued by a ship called the *Gellert* four days later. We wanted the captain of the *Gellert* to give young Dick a decent burial at sea. He refused. He took us back to Falmouth and we were arrested there."

"Ah, so you're an escaped prisoner!"

Captain Rutt shook his head wearily. "No, Sergeant. We didn't escape. We were put on trial. We were found guilty of murder. We were sentenced to death. Then our lawyer put in an appeal to the government. The Home Secretary said we'd suffered enough. He sentenced us to six months in prison. We came out two months ago."

The sergeant looked relieved. "So what's all this about a ghost, then? Dick Tomlin not satisfied with

36

the verdict, was he? Come back to haunt you?"

Captain Rutt sat at the table again, rested his elbows on the edge and looked across at the policeman. "That is what someone wants us to believe."

The sergeant's face remained blank. "So there's not a ghost, then?"

The sailor lowered his voice to a whisper. "It depends if you believe in ghosts or not. That's why I asked you. Do you believe in ghosts? If you do then there's no hope for me."

The policeman's face closed into a mask of red wrinkles as he thought about the problem. "I believe in God," he said. "And I believe in the Devil. But ghosts, sir . . . no. You goes to heaven or you goes to hell, but you doesn't hang around this world, does you? Stands to reason!"

Captain Rutt nodded. "Exactly. In that case there is someone out there trying to kill me."

"Have you any proof of this?" the sergeant asked, startled.

"He has already killed Josh Dudley and Will Hoon."

"The other men in the lifeboat?"

"That's right."

"How?"

"Josh Dudley found work as a dray man," the captain explained, "delivering beer on a horse-drawn wagon. He'd only been working a month when he took the horses out one foggy London night. A night just like tonight. He was trotting down the road when something leapt out from an alleyway and scared the

37

horses. They reared up in the air and then bolted. And you know what happens if you try to gallop down these cobbled streets?"

"You overturns," Sergeant Button said.

"Exactly. The beer wagon overturned and Dudley went crashing to the ground. Landed on his head. Half a dozen beer barrels rolled over him but they reckon he was dead before that."

The policeman sucked air between his yellow teeth. "Oooooh! Nasty accident. I remember now. Just before Christmas, wasn't it?"

Captain Rutt leaned forward. "Not an accident, Sergeant. Someone deliberately jumped out and frightened those horses."

"Any witnesses?" the policeman asked.

The little man nodded slowly. "Two. They said they saw the figure run out and wave his hands at the horses."

"And the description fitted the description of Dick Tomlin!" the policeman said. His face lit up as he thought he understood the problem.

But the captain shook his head. "If it had then I might have believed in the story of Tomlin's ghost. But no, this figure was covered from head to foot in bandages. Bloodstained bandages!"

The sergeant nodded. "Exactly! Tomlin's ghost!"

Rutt clenched his fists tight. "That is what you are meant to think," he said.

"I am?"

"Yes. If the police think a ghost scared those horses then the police won't go out looking for the real killer."

38

"Ah, I see," the sergeant said, disappointed. "So who did it?"

The captain shrugged one shoulder. "One of Tomlin's friends. One of his relatives? Whoever it was it wasn't a ghost. Remember, we don't believe in ghosts, Sergeant."

"No, sir. We don't. Still, it's a bit spooky all the same."

"It's not, Sergeant," the sailor said, his voice rising in temper. "It is simple human revenge. I knew that. Which was why I set off in search of Will Hoon. I had to warn him what was going on. He took a lot of finding. You see he'd heard about Dudley's death and he'd heard about the figure in the bloodstained bandages. He lost his nerve and went into hiding. Just last week I found him down by the docks."

"Alive?" the sergeant asked.

"Alive. But only just. The man had lost his nerve. He was drinking too much gin and he ended up in hospital. He was having terrible dreams. He really believed the figure in bandages was coming to get him. I think I might have saved him if I'd had time. But I left him sleeping in the Charity Hospital and promised to go back and see him the next day. When I went back he was dead."

The policeman's red face was turning pale. The only sound in the little room was the hissing of the gas lamp. Thick fog pawed at the outside of the window to the room and deadened any sounds.

Finally Rutt spoke. "He'd died of a fit, they said. But I saw Will Hoon's face before they took him away. It had an expression of terror. He'd been scared to death."

"By what?" the sergeant asked. His voice was hoarse.

"Witnesses said they woke up when Hoon started screaming. There was a dim night-light in the ward but they thought someone was trying to calm him down. They said it must have been a patient . . . because he was covered from head to toe in bandages. Bloodstained bandages."

Sergeant Button swallowed hard. "Did they find this patient? Question him?"

"There was no such patient in the hospital, the doctors said. And no one ever saw that figure again."

The policeman nodded. "So you think he'll find you next?"

Rutt's eyes shifted nervously towards the window. "Oh, he's found me, Sergeant. He must have been following me for some time. In fact I reckon I led him to Will Hoon's sick bed!"

The sergeant used the chewed end of his pencil to scratch his head. "So, why didn't he kill you?"

The red-rimmed eyes stared across. "Because he's leaving me till last. At the trial I admitted that I was the one who killed the lad. Now I have to suffer more than the other two. I've had to watch my two shipmates die . . . and now I have to wait for my turn. Don't you see, man, this avenger doesn't just want me to die . . . he wants me to suffer! Death would be a relief after the last two days I've spent. I can trust no one. That's the clever thing about the disguise . . . I don't know what my hunter looks like! He could be the man on the stairs or the man at the table in the

40

hotel. It could even be a woman – Tomlin's sister or his aunt. I just don't know. I scarcely dare to sleep. I'm at my wits' end. I can only think of one place I'll be safe. Here. In the police cells."

The sergeant tugged a watch from his pocket and looked at it. "Half-past eleven. I don't suppose it would do any harm to let you stay for the rest of the night. We have a free cell at the end."

"It's safe?"

The policeman attempted a jolly laugh. "I think we'd notice a bloke in bloodstained bandages wandering past the desk!"

Rutt didn't laugh. "I'll take it. Thank you, Sergeant."

The policeman rose stiffly and sifted through his keys. "Not often we get people asking to be locked up! Hah! Wait till I tell the lads."

The captain was standing by the door. He turned sharply. "Tell no one!"

Sergeant Button blinked. "No, sir! If that's what you want, sir!" He led the way down the dim corridor to the cell at the end and let the sailor into a bare room with a wooden plank bed and a grimy grey blanket. "Sleep tight!"

Rutt rattled the door to test the lock. He looked out through the small window. For the first time since he'd entered the police station his face was relaxed. The deep lines of worry were falling away and he looked younger.

"Thank you, Sergeant," he said.

The policeman grinned. "My pleasure, sir. I'll have one of the maids bring you a cup of tea and breakfast

41

in bed, eh? All part of the service," he chuckled until his chins wobbled.

Rutt managed a smile as Sergeant Button waddled back down to the desk.

Sergeant Button had been a policeman for thirty years. He'd seen a lot of strange sights. But this was the strangest.

His hand reached for the door to the entrance hall. In his thirty years he'd heard a lot of strange sounds – but none so eerie as the desperate scream that came from behind him. He turned slowly. There was a second scream more chilling than the first. Then, worst of all . . . an unearthly silence.

The policeman hurried back down the hall as fast as his ageing legs would carry him. He didn't need to check which cell the scream had come from. He knew. The cell key was still in his hand and he flung the door open.

Captain Edwin Rutt was lying on the bed with his knees drawn up to his chest. His lips were pulled back from his teeth and his eyes were saucer-wide. Eyes as lifeless as the glass eyes of a model in Madame Tussaud's. The eyes of a dead man.

There was a clattering of feet as policemen came running from all corners of the building. They strained to see past the bulky figure of the sergeant. Finally one pushed past and looked closely at the dead sailor.

"What happened, Sarge?"

The old policeman's face was as blank as the captain's.

"There's something in his hand," another officer

said.

"Bandage," the sergeant croaked. "It's bandage, isn't it?"

The policeman by the body looked up. "How did you know?" He tugged the scrap of material from the rigid hand of the captain. "And it's stained, Sergeant. Stained with blood!"

All Sergeant Button could say was, "And he didn't believe in ghosts, you know, he didn't believe in ghosts."

Ghostly revenge — FACT FILE

This incredible story was recorded by a ghost-hunter in 1920. The captain's fear of an avenging family rather than an avenging ghost is possible. It is also possible that the man died of fear in his cell. The only fantastic fact is then the appearance of the blood-stained bandage in his hand. Was this added to the story when it was re-told? Was someone trying to make the story more mysterious than it really was? Or is it a really ghostly story?

1. Voices from the grave

Stories about ghosts attacking living people are quite rare. Most ghosts are harmless to the living and hardly ever seem to notice the real world around them when they appear. However, there are many cases recorded where the ghost has tried to get justice for the death of their body by appearing to the living and telling their story.

2. Death in the barn

One of the most famous examples is the story known as The Red Barn Murder. In 1826 in Suffolk, England, young William Corder said he was taking his lover, Maria Marten, to London to marry her. After a few letters, written for Maria by William, her parents heard nothing more from her. Then her step-mother had horrific dreams. She said Maria appeared to her and claimed that she had not gone to London. In fact she had never left Suffolk. Maria's spirit said William had murdered her and buried her body in the Red Barn. When her father searched the barn he found the body just where Maria's ghost had said it was. William Corder was brought to trial and hanged.

The story of the ghost's revenge became a best-selling book and popular play for the next hundred years.

3. Delayed vengeance
Sometimes ghosts appear to take revenge for things that happen to them after they have died! The San Francisco Examiner newspaper described such a case in 1981. Farmer George Walsingham found some old bones on his land and decided to burn them rather than give them a proper burial. Shortly afterwards he heard laughter, screams and wailing all over his house. Footprints appeared alongside him as he crossed a muddy field. A hand appeared in the air and shook his daughter's shoulder. Finally, blood dripped from the ceiling onto the dinner table while he had guests. Tests later showed that it was human blood. Walsingham eventually gave up and moved out.

4. Disturbing the dead
In most cultures any attempt to disturb the dead is considered to be both disrespectful and unwise. One such story tells of the mummified Egyptian princess Ammon Ra who lay peacefully for over three thousand years until she was dug up in 1910. The young man who unearthed Ammon Ra tried to sell her to the collector, Douglas Murray, but died before he could collect the payment. Murray blew his own arm

off in a shoooting accident shortly after collecting the princess but survived to take her back to England. He seemed to have terrible luck when he reached England and decided to give the mummy to a museum. The musuem became so cursed by sudden deaths they offered to sell Ammon Ra to an American collector. The story goes that the avenging mummy was loaded secretly onto a ship but, halfway across the Atlantic, the ship struck an iceberg. The ship's name was the Titanic.

5. A ghost that travels
Elsie Marshall, a vicar's daughter, was killed in 1893 by an outlaw gang in China. She did not return to haunt her killers – she had gone to China to be a missionary, so perhaps she forgave them! However, she has crossed the world to haunt the library of her old home in Blackheath, London.

4. "We will torment you . . ."

When someone utters a curse can it really work? Can people truly suffer horrific visions and dreadful luck because they are under a lifelong curse? The case of Myles Phillipson and his wife seems to prove that such things do exist. How else can their story be explained?

27 December 1687 – Calgarth Hall

My dear Uncle James,

I am turning to you as my last hope. You are my godfather – the nearest thing I have to a family since my father and mother died. Please don't lie to me like the others. Tell me the truth about the screaming skulls. Please. Before I go mad.

Ever since I was a child my parents sent me to stay with you at Christmas. I never knew why. Now that they are dead I decided to spend Christmas here at Calgarth Hall. I should have known something was wrong when the butler, Cromarty, tried to persuade me to leave. "Why should I?" I asked.

He muttered something about a Christmas ghost but wouldn't tell me any more. The other servants said they never stayed at the Hall on Christmas night. They left me here alone. To my shame I actually thought it might be fun to meet a ghost.

When the last one left for the night, I locked the doors, read a book for a while in front of the fire. But the fire burned badly. A draught blew smoke back down the chimney. The cold and the smoke drove me to bed before ten o'clock.

It was peaceful without the servants there. I fell asleep quickly and I dreamed. And in my dream I saw a man and a woman. They had rope around their necks and the rope was choking them. As they struggled for air they gave the most hideous screams.

Their eyes bulged and their faces were purple. I woke suddenly. The bedroom was dark. The fire had gone out. For all the cold in the bedroom I found my night-shirt soaked with sweat. But worst of all the screaming continued even though I was now wide awake.

I fumbled for a flint and struck a light. The screams were louder now. My hands were shaking so much that the candle cast crazy shadows on the wall as I crept to the door. I stepped into the corridor. The screams were coming from the stairs. Two choking screams.

I reached the top of the stairs and the noise stopped

suddenly. I looked down and there, on the first landing sat two ordinary, eyeless skulls grinning up at me. The only unusual thing was that one of the skulls had long hair attached . . . like a woman's hair. Somehow I knew that it was the skulls that had made the noise.

I couldn't bring myself to pick them up. I backed away and fled to my room. I locked the door – though God knows what I thought that would do. I lit more candles and tried to start the fire. I stared at the bedroom door and waited till dawn.

The footsteps on the stairs came with the first light. A soft, slow tread. The third step creaked as it always did. I jumped out of bed and tore open the curtains. The pearl-grey sky was the most welcome sight I'd seen.

The footsteps had reached the landing where the skulls were waiting. My guest paused. Now I had a new fear that even the locked door wouldn't keep my visitor out of the room. I snatched at one of the old swords that decorate the room. I believe a great uncle had used it during the war against Cromwell.

The footsteps started again and I heard them reach the top of the stairs. They paused again. In the silence I could imagine my visitor deciding which way to turn. Then a step – two steps – three steps. They were headed my way! I raised the sword above my head and waited for my visitor to walk through the door.

The steps stopped outside the door. I watched, my mouth as dry as the ashes in the hearth as the door handle turned. The door creaked as someone, or something, pushed against it and found it locked. I could hear breathing now. It sounded like the loud, creaking breaths of an old man.

"Who's there?" I cried. My voice was as choked as the screams in my nightmare.

"It's Cromarty, sir. I've brought your morning dish of chocolate. May I come in?"

I almost swooned but managed to unlock the door and fall back onto the bed. The servant looked at me. I'll swear there was amusement in his sunken, colourless eyes. "Perhaps it was unwise of you to have spent the night alone, sir. You look as if you've had a restless night."

"Skulls," I said.

"Ah, the screaming skulls. Yes, sir. I'll put them back in the cupboard."

"Cupboard?" I squawked. "Throw them out!"

"Excuse me, sir," the butler said. "Your late father, Mr Myles, tried that. The screams haunt the house every night until the skulls are brought back. Mr Myles had a special cupboard built in the library. They are happy to remain there . . . except on Christmas night, sir."

"Why Christmas night?" I asked.

"I really can't say, sir."

"Where did they come from?" I demanded.

"It is not my place to repeat the stories about them, sir," he went on quietly.

"Why didn't you tell me about them?" I asked.

He buried his long head in his withered shoulders as a sort of shrug. "I tried to warn you, sir may remember. Perhaps sir would not have believed me if he had not seen it with his own two eyes. Now, sir, may I replace the sword in its place on the wall. I can

50

assure you that you do not need to defend yourself against me."

I realised I was waving the thing in front of me as I spoke to him. I threw it on the bed.

So, Uncle. I am an utter fool. Everyone seems to know about the skulls. No one will tell me their story. Please help. Where did they come from?

Your grateful nephew,

Andrew

3 January 1688, Enderby Manor

My dear Andrew,

I do feel I have let you down. You are right. Someone should have told you about the skulls. But believe me, no one did so because we were trying to be kind! The story is a grisly and unhappy one. Your father and your mother, it must be said, come out of it in a very poor light. It is wrong to speak unkindly about the dead – but I believe it is my sad duty to do so now.

The story began twenty-five years or so ago. Before you were born, of course. King Charles II had just returned to the throne after the wars against Cromwell. A lot of landowners had their land taken from them by Cromwell. The King restored it to those who had fought for him. That still left many estates in the King's hands. He sold them off very cheaply. Your father bought one.

The estate was fine but the house that went with it was poor. Your father and mother knew exactly where they wanted their new house built. But that piece of land was owned by an old farming couple, Kraster and Dorothy Cook. Their family had lived on the land for centuries. They would not sell the land at any price.

Your father was furious. Your mother persuaded him that if he couldn't get the Cooks' land by fair means then they should get it by foul.

I am sorry to say this, but the plan was quite despicable. First they invited the Cooks to a Christmas party. The old couple were shy and quiet people. They probably felt uncomfortable with your father's fine friends. Still, they went to the party. At one moment in the party your father suddenly cried out to Kraster Cook, "Ah! I see you are admiring our fine silver bowl!"

The old man turned red. He was probably doing no such thing, but everyone heard your father's comment and remembered it.

The party finished and the Cooks went home. They were awakened next morning by soldiers at the door. Kraster and Dorothy were marched off to jail . . . and no one would tell them why. It was only when they arrived in court a month later that they discovered they were being accused of stealing the silver bowl from your parents' Christmas table.

Your mother went into the witness stand and told how she noticed both of the Cooks looking enviously at the bowl during the Christmas dinner. Then two of your parents' servants said they had seen the Cooks lingering in the dining room when everyone else was in the hall dancing. What really condemned the old couple was the soldiers who swore that they had searched the Cooks' house and found the bowl hidden under a bed.

Of course we can see now that they were all lying at your father's request. The Cooks were too shocked to put up any kind of defence. At the time everyone believed they were guilty.

Certainly the judge did. He sentenced them to be hanged.

That sentence seemed to rouse Dorothy Cook from her shock. She turned to where your parents sat and screeched, "As sure as there is a just God, Myles Phillipson, you and your wife will be damned for ever for your actions. Neither you nor your family will prosper. Your friendship will prove fatal and those that you love will die in pain and sorrow. There will be no happiness, in your old house or your new, for my husband and I will be with you night and day. We will torment you. As long as you live you shall never be rid of us."

She was dragged off to prison. They tried to appeal. But finally they were hanged . . . on Christmas Day, as it happened.

Your parents took the Cooks' farm and tore down their cottage. Then they built Calgarth Hall. By the following Christmas they were living there and held a great Christmas party to celebrate. As your father's best friend I was invited.

I remember watching your mother leave the room to fetch some jewels. A few minutes later she rushed back into the dining room screaming. She claimed that she had seen two skulls perched on the banisters grinning at her!

One was a woman's with long hair hanging down. The other was clearly a man's. The men drew their swords and we rushed out. There were no skulls on the banisters – we climbed the dim, candle-lit stairs and saw the skulls had moved. They were sitting on the landing now, their mouths open as if they wanted to speak . . . or scream. They were silent.

I stepped forward and prodded at them with my sword. They were real skulls, not phantoms. "This is some foolish trick," I said and scooped one up on the point of my sword. The skulls were thrown into the farmyard and left for the crows to pick at.

But in the deepest, darkest part of the night we were shaken from our beds by those dreadful strangled screams. We tumbled out of our rooms and dashed to the landing. The skulls were back. As soon as someone laid eyes on them the screaming stopped.

Most of the guests packed their cases and left Calgarth that very night. We threw the skulls in the farm pond this time. Next night they were back again. Word of the skulls went around. Calgarth Hall was said to be cursed. And the curse seemed to work. No one wanted to do business with your father and he lost most of his fortune.

You were born the next year. The screaming skulls remained quiet so long as they stayed in the house. Your father had a special cupboard built for them. Only he held the key . . . yet that next Christmas they were there again, scaring away the few guests who had dared to come to the Christmas party.

Of course your parents started sending you away for Christmas. As you grew up you knew nothing of the curse.

I hoped that the curse would die with your parents. I didn't see the need to tell you the story. I hoped you'd never hear the tale of the screaming skulls. I was foolish and wrong. I see that now. You found out in the most terrifying way imaginable.

Twenty years ago I would never have believed in such foolishness as curses. But your father's fortune is all but gone now.

I'll pray for you, my boy. May the Phillipson luck change for the better.

Let me know if I can help you in any way.

Your loving godfather,

James

The screaming skulls — FACT FILE

1. Pursued by poverty

Calgarth Hall used to stand near Lake Windermere in the English Lake District. It is gone now. In her curse Dorothy Cook predicted, "Neither you nor your family will prosper." Not only did Myles Phillipson lose most of his fortune but his son, Andrew, lost what was left. Calgarth Hall passed out of the hands of the Phillipson family and each generation became poorer and poorer. The last Phillipson died, a tramp, in a ditch. The curse seems to have worked. But the screaming skulls could well have been conjured up as the revenge of a living relative, or friend, of the dead Cooks. No one saw the skulls actually scream. Someone could have placed the skulls, then hid and screamed until people came running. A man-servant in the house was suspected of such a trick when the skulls first appeared. However, it is strange that Dorothy Cook said the Phillipson family would be ruined . . . and they were. That is harder to explain.

2. Lucky skulls

Skull stories have been repeated since the Romans ruled Britain. The native tribes, the Celts, believed that the head of a dead person was especially precious. Heads of dead enemies, for example, would be nailed to the walls of a Celtic warrior's house. They brought luck. One popular legend described how the Celtic hero Bran asked for his head to be cut off when he died. It was carried around like a good- luck *charm by the Celtic army. When the head was stolen after twenty years, the Celts were defeated.*

3. Death wish
Theophilus Broome died in 1670 in Chilton Cantelo, Somerset. As he lay dying he asked that his skull should be kept at the farmhouse where he had spent a happy life. His relatives tried to bury the skull with the body. Screaming noises disturbed them every night until his wish was granted. The skull can be seen in the farmhouse to this day. Is this a story that Kraster Cook's avengers heard and decided to copy?

4. Using her head
One of the most famous British Screaming Skulls is at Bettiscombe Manor in Dorset. No one can agree on the true history of the skull, which has its jaw missing. It is said to have belonged to a slave or a girl who was imprisoned and killed. Scientists have said it is in fact the remains of a prehistoric woman. Whoever she (or he) is, the skull does not seem to demand the same respect as other family skulls. Some people remember it being played with by children as a toy . . . others claim that visiting ghosts took the skull and used it to play a game of bowls!

5. Transatlantic skull
Skull stories crossed the Atlantic to America. The Pew family of France kept the skull of an ancestor. They nicknamed it 'Ferdinand'. They took it with them when they settled in America in the 1680s. They claimed that when Ferdinand was taken out of the

family home it screamed – if it ever screamed inside the home then that was a sign that one of the family was about to die. One member of the family showed Ferdinand to a surgeon. The surgeon believed it was in fact the skull of a native American Indian and that the Pew family had obtained it after they had landed. Perhaps they wanted to impress their neighbours with a mysterious story!

5. "I order you, most evil spirit . . ."

When story-tellers and film-makers first began producing horror stories they often set the scene in a lonely old castle. But do such places really exist? According to the diary of a French nobleman who called himself 'X' there are some places that are every bit as frightening as fiction . . .

Calvados Castle, Normandy – 1875

13 October 1875

No one in the castle knows about this diary I have started tonight. It may be useful as evidence when I catch the criminal who is trying to scare us from our home. The writing will help to pass the time during the sleepless nights. The nights when we are afraid to sleep.

But I must begin at the beginning. I don't know who will read this diary or when. I don't even know

59

how long this terror will go on.

Let me begin with the scene of our drama then go on to list the cast. Lastly I will record the action.

The scene is Calvados Castle. It stands in the finest apple orchards of northern France – a grey and gloomy wart on the beautiful face of the countryside. Cold draughts rattle at the doors; heavy shutters try to keep them out – they keep out the sunshine too. Candles quiver in the chill air and shadows hide the snuffling, shuffling, whispering creatures of the night. There are corners where even the castle cats are afraid to go.

Calvados was built five hundred years ago. It has been in the hands of my family ever since. I could leave – but the honour of my family prevents me. I must stay. It is my home. I love it.

What people have lived – and died – here? Who can count? And how did they die? Who knows? We keep the wine in the cellars. But, as for the dungeons with their rats and their terrible secrets . . . no one goes there now.

The place must have been filled with torch-light and warmth and happy humans at some time in its past. Now there are just eight of us.

I live here with my wife and son. His teacher is a monk . . . Father Dominic. We have a coachman, his name is Emile, and three maids. Their names are not important. They may not be with us much longer. They are afraid of the noises.

There have always been noises in the castle. The crackling of the fires and the wind whining through the shutters, floors creaking and the rumbling of draughts in the chimneys.

But that first night we all knew it was not one of the friendly, familiar sounds of the castle talking to us. It was almost a human sound. The sound of someone weeping.

At first I thought it might be one of the maids. I rose from bed and pulled a dressing gown on. "What is it?" my wife asked.

"I'll go and see. The foolish girl can't keep us awake all night," I said.

"She sounds so sad," my wife replied. "Don't be too angry with her."

I picked up a candle and opened the door into the corridor. The air seemed icier than ever, though the worst of winter is still a month or two away. The candle showed little – the blackness seemed so thick out there. I moved towards the stairway of the west tower. A door opened and Father Dominic appeared.

We did not speak. He simply joined me at the foot of the stairs and we began to climb. The father's candle threw my shadow on the wall ahead of me. The sobbing grew louder as I climbed and seemed to echo down the spiral stairway.

I reached the door on the first landing and waited for Father Dominic to join me. Slowly I stretched out a hand towards the black iron handle.

As I touched the cold metal there was a great crash that shook the door. I jumped back and almost knocked the monk down the stairs.

"Sorry, Father!" I gasped.

He blinked and wiped sweat off his bald head with a trembling hand. This time I was not going to be

61

timid. I stepped forward, grasped the handle firmly and threw the door open. A blast of air blew out my candle but Father Dominic's stayed alight.

We re-lit my candle and stepped carefully into the room. It was silent. It was in darkness until we entered.

And it was empty. It has not been used for some time. A stripped bed and old chair stood against one wall. Whoever had been wailing had vanished.

Father Dominic began to mutter a prayer. The air in the room seemed to stir as he mumbled the words.

I backed out of the room. "Did you recognise her voice?" I asked Father Dominic. "Was it one of the maids?"

"I don't know," he admitted as we slowly descended to the corridor below. Four figures were waiting for us. Emile and the three maids. The monk exchanged a silent glance with me then spoke quickly to the servants. "Have any of you maids been in the tower tonight?"

They stared back wide-eyed, their skins pale as a winter moon. "No, Father," one muttered.

I turned and stalked back to my room angrily. "A silly joke," I said to my wife, then pulled the cover over me and closed my eyes.

There were no more noises that night. But the simple terror of that voice was as haunting as a cry from Hell. I fell asleep shortly before dawn.

In the morning light Father Dominic and I examined the room again. "Perhaps there is a secret door," he said slowly as he examined the wooden panels closely. "The girl could have screamed . . .

then, when we entered, she slipped out through the door, down a hidden passage and was waiting for us when we went back down."

Father Dominic has a great imagination. Normally I would have mocked his foolish idea . . . but I could think of nothing better. It was the likeliest explanation. The other servants would not betray her. They all hate me. Even my son hates me.

For the past week the performance has been repeated every night. I agreed with the Father that I should keep this diary. What I did not tell him was that I will put down my pen, leave my room and set a trap. I cannot tell him what that trap is. After all, he may be part of the plot to frighten me.

14 October 1875

I am so tired. My night was disturbed again. When the screams came they were louder than ever. I was already dressed and jumped from my bed so that I would be first on the scene.

I rushed through the cold corridors so quickly that my candle almost blew out. When I reached the bottom of the tower staircase I dropped to my knees and examined my trap. For I had stretched a piece of silk across the stairs. It was unbroken.

I was not too disappointed. If the girl was running down a secret stairway then she could well have gone back that way. I hurried up the stairs. The near-invisible silk placed across the door was also undamaged.

No one had entered or left the room. But there was someone in there. The sobs were those of someone broken hearted – the screams that mingled with them were from a person with a tortured body. I reached for the handle. The crash sounded against the door as it always did. This time I did not step back. I lunged forward and tore the door open.

The screams seemed to disappear out of the shuttered window. The room had five walls as well as the one with the door in it. Each wall was guarded by a piece of silk thread. I knelt on the rough stone floor and looked at each piece in turn. If she had slipped out of a door in one of the walls then the broken silk would tell me which one.

I found the five lengths of thread. Each one was unbroken.

I cursed and left the room. As I closed the door behind me, I'll swear it came from the room. It was not the usual crying – it may have been laughter.

15 October 1875

No screams tonight. The spirit has turned its evil upon Father Dominic. I heard a crash in the room below me. The father's room. I climbed wearily from my bed.

When I reached the bottom of the stairs, Father Dominic was waiting for me. "Ah, my lord, please come to my room at once!" The man had ugly eyes that were bulging and watery. Tonight the candle lit something deeper in the black pupils. Something I have seen in soldiers about to go into battle. Something called fear.

"What's wrong?" I asked. "You look as if you've seen a ghost."

He nodded dumbly and began to walk back to his room. He stopped at the door and looked over his shoulder at me. I took it as a sign to follow him.

His room was in great disorder. A chair that was usually fastened to the floor had turned over. The candlesticks and religious statues had been thrown from the mantelpiece and lay broken in the hearth. Pages from a book were shredded on the floor.

Father Dominic stared at the remains of a shattered plaster crucifix and began to explain. "I heard a tapping. I struck a light. I saw the candlestick rising and falling on the mantelpiece. Some unseen hand was making it rise and fall."

"I have heard of such things," I said. "They are spirits known as poltergeists. They have great force."

The man's eyes bulged. "The candlestick swept everything from the mantelpiece then the spirit turned to the chair. It began rocking. It's so heavy I couldn't move it if I tried. At last it rocked so far it fell to the floor!" He picked up the damaged book. "The Bible – it even tore my Bible."

Maybe someone was playing these tricks using hidden ropes like a fairground conjurer. Then the floor began to tremble underneath our feet. The whole room was shaking. Somewhere up above a woman screamed.

It felt as if the castle was under attack and that an iron cannonball was beating against the walls. Now I would catch the trickster, I decided.

"The hall," I said to Father Dominic. "Call everyone to the hall!"

It took no time at all for the household to assemble.

They were already awake. They stood there shivering, my wife, pale and shaking, my son dazed and asleep on his feet, Father Dominic, his fat lips moving in prayer, Emile, looking wildly around for some clue as to where the attack was coming from. The three maids clung together for comfort.

Still that thumping. Regular beating like a drum. Louder and louder. My wife clamped her hands over her ears and closed her eyes as if in pain.

Everyone was present. That was when I realised the force was in the walls of the old castle itself. The household seemed to be waiting for me to make an announcement. I had to shout to make myself heard. "This is clearly an evil spirit," I told them. "But don't worry, this sort of being doesn't usually harm humans. Go back to your beds. I will deal with it tomorrow."

I could see they are wondering how I will manage this. They hate me – but they believe me and trust me.

As I left the hall there was the sound of heavy footsteps running up the corridor. Too heavy and too fast to be human. I didn't bother to follow. Then a slow fading of the sounds till the air trembled with the silence.

And, in the silence, the distant sound of laughter.

18 October 1875

Peace. The priest from the town came last night.

We took out all our religious relics – the prayer books, crosses, paintings and statues. We placed them in full view while the priest began the exorcism.

"Adjure te, spiritus nequissime, per Deum

omnipotentem . . ." he recited. I order you, most evil spirit, in the name of almighty God.

The whole service lasted half an hour. And the hearts of the household rose like Father Dominic's candlestick.

And like Father Dominic's candlestick they were dashed to the earth soon afterwards.

We said farewell to the priest then returned to the hall to collect our religious relics. They had disappeared. From the torn scraps of Father Dominic's Bible to the heavy silver cross from the castle chapel.

We retired to bed last night and waited for the spirit to return. At last we fell asleep. This morning we agreed that the spirit had truly left us. Yet it had one last trick to play.

As my wife sat at her table writing, the invisible hand dropped all the religious relics in front of her. With a final burst of noise it left.

Tonight the air in the old castle is cleaner. We can all feel it. The spirit has left the castle to us . . . and to the old ghosts that have always wandered its rooms.

Exorcism — FACT FILE

Mr X who wrote the diary was probably right – and wrong! Spirits which disturb a place with noises and throwing objects around have been widely reported. They are known as poltergeists.

However, psychic investigators believe that there is usually a teenage boy or girl in the troubled house. Their theory is that some teenagers have a troublesome force inside that they cannot control. Most don't even realise they are to blame for the disturbances. Mr X didn't seem to suspect that his son may have been the centre of the destructive happenings.

The force, then, was more likely to be from a human than an evil spirit.

Did you know . . .

1. Ancient ceremonies
Exorcism has been practised since ancient times. Babylonians had special priests who would destroy a clay or wax model of a demon. This was expected to destroy the actual demon. The Ancient Egyptians and Greeks had similar ceremonies.

2. Promises, promises
The word 'exorcism' is from the Ancient Greek word exousia which means 'promise'. The words don't 'drive out' the devil; they make the spirit 'promise' to behave itself.

3. Alternative medicine

The ancients also believed that evil spirits could be the cause of illness. If someone fell ill they might well have called in an exorcist rather than a doctor. A 'Witch Doctor' or a 'Medicine Man' would be a little of both.

4. Powerful words

Many religions around the world still practise exorcism. Sometimes this can take the form of friendly persuasion – politely suggesting that the spirit should go away. Others are great ceremonies; the Roman Catholic Church, for example, has a service called Rituale Romanum which was first used in 1614 and uses Latin verses. Presumably evil spirits still speak Latin!

5. Spirit levellers

Amateur exorcists have harsher ways of dealing with devils. If a person is believed to be possessed by a devil then their body may be tortured in the hope that the pain will drive the evil spirit away! The victim may be beaten, starved, suffer electric shocks, foul smells or disgusting medicines. But can a spirit feel pain?

6. Frightening vocation

Some priests specialise in exorcisms. The Reverend J. R. Nesmith of London has carried out hundreds of such ceremonies. He once described entering a house where servants had been scared away by a haunting spirit. "I said a few prayers then the figure of a girl appeared. She was in Victorian dress. The three people with me either saw her or sensed that she was there. I asked her what she wanted and she said she was unable to rest because of her unhappy life. I prayed that she would find rest, exorcised the building, and there were no more problems after that." This is a very unusual case since ghosts seem to exist in a world of their own. They do not often notice humans, let alone talk to them.

7. No certain cure

Exorcism does not always work. The Sheriff family in Yorkshire were troubled by an old woman who appeared in the toilet and waved a white stick at the family – neighbours said it was the last owner of the house, Mrs Nelson, who had died in the toilet. Noises and objects moving disturbed the Sheriffs as they tried to sleep. A Catholic "blessing" failed to stop Mrs Nelson. The disturbances put 12-year-old Michael into hospital in a state of shock after his family found him floating two metres above his bed! The family moved house . . . but a new ghost was waiting to torment them. It was only after they moved a second time that they found peace.

6. "Six foot under now."

Some people will do anything for money. Morality, faith, and cleanliness of the soul can all be sacrificed for a handful of jangling silver coins. But sometimes, just sometimes, the victims of these people have the final say . . .

The Forth Valley, Scotland – 1818

The girl was twenty years old. She would have been pretty but the tears made her eyes swollen and red. They trickled onto the freshly filled grave. "Davie," she moaned. "Oh, my Davie."

The sun had set and the cold moon turned the grey gravestones to silver. Two men stepped from the shadows. One well-dressed, slim and young. The other shorter, a thick, well-muscled body wrapped in a rough wool jacket. "Ah, young lady," the tall one said gently. "You should be home in front of a fire."

She looked up through tear-filled eyes and rubbed

71

the back of her hand across her running nose. "Oh, I can't bear to leave my poor Davie," she sniffed.

"He was your love?" the young man asked kindly.

"We were to be married this summer . . . then he took a fever and died suddenly," she whined.

"That's interesting," the young man said to his companion.

"Interesting?" the girl said sharply.

"Sorry, dear young lady. But I am a doctor. Of course I am interested in illness – I study it in the hope of finding a cure," he said smoothly.

"I see, Doctor . . ."

"My name is Liston," the thin young man said. "This is my . . . servant. Mr Crouch."

The girl nodded at him then turned back to arrange flowers over the dark soil. "I wish you could have treated Davie," she sighed.

"I do know that I'll be treating you soon, young lady, if you stay in the damp night air much longer. You'll make yourself ill," Doctor Liston said.

"I don't care. I don't care if I die," she said and pushed out her lips in a pout.

"Now, now!" the young doctor comforted. "You have your whole life ahead of you. There are worse things than life without Davie, you know."

"No, I don't know," she said pitifully. "What could be worse?"

Doctor Liston took a step towards her and said, "I have heard that there are body-snatchers in the area. No sooner would you be dead and buried than you would be snatched from your grave. And do you know what would happen to your body?"

The girl tried to say, 'No', but the word wouldn't form in her fear-tightened throat.

"They would take it to the hospital and cut it into pieces, wouldn't they, Mr Crouch?"

"Aye, tiny little pieces," Crouch agreed. "They try to find out how every part of the body works, don't they, Doctor Liston?"

"They do," Liston said with a glance at the stocky man. He turned back to the girl. "Imagine meeting your Davie in the afterlife with your body in pieces. Davie wouldn't like that, would he?"

The young woman shook her head dumbly. "So, why don't you run off home and keep yourself in one piece for dear Davie, eh?"

He held out his hand and helped her to her feet. "B-b-bodysnatchers . . ." she stammered. "D-D-Davie?"

"Ahh. You are worried that these evil men might come for your loved one?" Doctor Liston asked.

She nodded.

"Dig him up?"

Her eyes widened.

"Pop him into a sack?"

Her mouth hung open.

"Have ye got no one to guard the body?" Crouch asked.

"I never thought," she whispered.

"Be sure to arrange it tomorrow," the young man suggested.

The girl once more nodded her head fast as a starling's wing. "What about tonight?"

"Ah, that's a problem, isn't it, Crouch?" the doctor said.

"A problem."

"Of course, it's a fine night. No doubt Mr Crouch and I could help you out until you've made arrangements."

"We could," Crouch agreed. "I could run down to the tavern at Rosyth and fetch us some brandy," he offered.

"Have you enough money?" the doctor asked.

"Aye, there's a problem," the smaller man said slapping at empty pockets.

"I've a guinea!" the girl offered.

"We couldn't . . . " Doctor Liston said.

"Well, we could always pay her back tomorrow," Crouch suggested.

The young man spread his hands wide. "If that is agreeable to the young lady . . . then, yes we accept. Come back here at first light. We'll see the grave is well looked after – and we'll repay the guinea," he said, slipping the gold coin from her grasp. "Now you get home into the warmth, young lady. Sleep well."

With the two men following her with their eyes, she set off down the path. Then she stopped and turned. "How can I ever thank you?" she asked.

"Think nothing of it, dear lady. Our reward will be to see you well and happy tomorrow. Goodnight!" the doctor said with a wave.

The girl disappeared into the distance. The two men stood perfectly still for several minutes. An owl hooted from the graveyard yew tree and bats flickered their silhouettes against the three-quarter moon. At last Doctor Liston moved. He rubbed his hands together briskly. "Where is the equipment, Crouch?"

"In the trees, Doc."

"Fetch it. We've wasted enough time . . . I thought she'd never go!" Crouch brought a bag from the shadows of the trees and took out two shovels with wooden handles, and a length of rope.

The two men worked quickly and as a well-trained team. They were silent as moles and the coffin was uncovered in ten minutes. Crouch dropped into the hole and used a short lever to pull off the coffin lid. He looped the rope around poor Davie's still body and Liston pulled it carefully out of the grave. As the doctor tucked the corpse neatly into a sack, Crouch already had the grave half-filled again.

The doctor helped him to finish the job then replaced the flowers on the top. When the girl returned she would never know she was shedding her tears over an empty wooden box.

Liston picked up the tools. For the first time since the girl had left he spoke. "What are you doing, Crouch?"

"Just picking a flower for my buttonhole," the shorter man said. He grinned a black-toothed grin as he selected a fresh rose-bud and slipped it into the lapel of his dark woollen jacket. Then he picked up the sack and hurried down the graveyard path after his partner.

The men reached the road and looked towards the village. "Should we risk going through the village?" Liston asked. There were lights at the windows of the poor cottages but no one on the street.

"Aye," Crouch growled. "We still have the lassie's guinea. That should buy us a few drinks at the tavern.

We don't have to wait for the Surgeons' College to pay us for the body. How much will we get for wee Davie anyway?"

"Ten pounds at least," the young doctor chuckled.

"And what do we do with him while we go to the inn? Take him with us? Prop him up in a chair and buy him a drink with his lassie's money?" Crouch giggled.

"Ah, no, he may be a handsome young lad. I don't want any competition. I want Mary all to myself. Let's away and see her," Liston said. "Just tuck Davie down in the ditch there. No one'll come along this way tonight."

Crouch did as his partner asked and the two men strolled down to the warm glowing lights of the inn.

"Evening, Mary, my lovely," Liston said as he came through the door.

The tavern was little more than a front room of a cottage but a fire glowed cheerfully enough in the hearth and Mary kept the tables clean and the floor covered in fresh sawdust.

The young woman stood behind a table that served as a bar. "So the bad penny's turned up again, has it?" she said severely.

"What's that supposed to mean?" Liston asked with an expression of mock pain.

"It means that I haven't seen you for two weeks and you promised me some ribbons from Edinburgh."

"Ah, Mary, you deserve better than ribbons." He snatched the rose from his partner's button hole and offered it to the girl.

"A rose," she said. "Roses are common. Why Ellen Duncan had roses like this for poor Davie's grave.

That's a lad from the village that died, you know. In here drinking last week, six foot under now."

Liston gave Mary his most charming smile. "Tell you what . . . I'll bring you a new silk dress. I'll have plenty of money soon. Come here and let me measure you!" Liston said.

The woman was just about to make a playful reply to the young doctor's flirting when a cry of "Ahoy there!" came from outside the door.

Mary's face glowed with pleasure. "That's my brother, Jock!" she cried.

The door swung open and a sailor stood there dusting his hands. "Mary! You'll never guess what I saw just now!"

"Come in, Jock, and close the door," she said, tugging at his arm and kissing him quickly on the cheek. She sat him at a table and poured beer into a jar. Mary placed the glowing poker into the beer until it bubbled and hissed. "Now, tell us, what did you just see?"

The sailor looked across at Liston and Crouch. "Be wary, sirs, but I think there are thieves in the area. I was walking down the lane when I saw two men with sacks . . . one large sack and one small."

He supped at the hot ale while Crouch asked, "Where did these men go?"

"I don't know," Jock admitted. "They dropped the sacks into the ditch and I went to see what they'd hidden. By the time I found the big sack the men had disappeared. I think they've maybe gone for a cart to carry their loot."

"Ooooh! Jock! You think the sack is full of loot?"

Mary gasped.

"Bound to be. Not silver or gold – the sack didn't rattle when I shook it," Jock said.

"You shook it?" Liston said flatly.

"Aye. Something soft. I have a feeling it could be some kind of material," the sailor said.

"Jockeeee!" Mary said excitedly and clapped her hands. "I need a new dress. Maybe we could sneak a piece . . ."

"I'll buy you a dress," Liston said urgently. "I promised."

The sailor looked over his ale mug at the doctor. "I can well look after my own sister's clothes, thank you, sir," he said stiffly.

"So, you'll fetch this material for me . . . before you report it to the constable?" Mary asked.

"No one'll miss a little cloth," her brother said with a wink. "I've got the sack outside."

"Let me see it!" she cried. "I want to see it now!"

The sailor drained his mug and went to the door. Liston and Crouch sat with their hands locked around their own mugs, stonier than the flagstones on the floor.

Jock turned and looked at the two men. "I see you two gentlemen are friends of Mary. I trust you'll not breathe a word of what's in the sack."

"Not a word," Liston said.

"Aye . . . I mean no!" Crouch agreed. "Not a single word."

Jock reached around the doorpost, gripped the sack and dragged it over the threshold.

The top of the sack was tied with a string. Jock

unfastened it carefully while Mary twisted her apron in her excited hands. "I hope it's my colour," she whimpered.

"Dammit, somebody strong fastened this," the sailor cursed.

"Aren't I lucky, Doctor Liston?" she sighed.

Liston looked at Crouch and mumbled, "Dead lucky."

Finally Jock pulled out a pocket knife and sliced through the string. "I hope it's white," Mary said.

"It will be," Crouch replied.

The sailor gripped the bottom of the sack, lifted it high in the air and let the contents tumble on the sawdust floor.

An hour later, when Liston and Crouch trudged miserable and empty-handed back to the city, Mary was still screaming.

Bodysnatching — FACT FILE

A doctor called Robert Christison was one of Doctor
Liston's students from 1817 to 1820. Many years later
he became a leading surgeon. As Sir Robert
Christison he wrote his life story. In his book he gave
many examples of Liston's life and bodysnatching
adventures. If his stories are to be believed, Sir Robert
had obviously taken part in many of the raids himself.

1. Gruesome record

Liston was a famous surgeon. It was said that he
could amputate a leg faster than any other doctor in
Scotland – 28 seconds was his record . . . though he
once cut off a leg so quickly that he cut off three of his
assistant's fingers at the same time! Liston could have
paid people to snatch bodies for his work, yet he
seemed to enjoy taking part himself. He was
immensely strong and this helped him in his gruesome
work. In 1820 he was caught by grave guards with
two adult bodies. Liston merely tucked one body
under each arm and ran off to freedom!

2. Demand for bodies

For many centuries doctors have cut up bodies to find
out how they work. They have done this since the time
of the Ancient Greeks. But seventeenth-century
Britain did not like the idea of people being cut up
after death. Laws were passed which stated that the
only bodies which could go to doctors for experiments
were the bodies of criminals. There was, therefore, a

shortage of legal bodies. Bodysnatchers supplied doctors with illegal ones by taking them from fresh graves. Liston and Crouch were two of the most successful bodysnatchers in Scottish history.

3. Body of evidence

The two most infamous bodysnatchers were Burke and Hare . . . However, they never snatched a single body! They ran a lodging house in Edinburgh for the poor. When they found a poor person alone they would offer them a bed for the night. . . then smother them to death and sell the body. Burke and Hare weren't really bodysnatchers, they were murderers. They were caught when they killed a popular local boy. In 1829 Burke was hanged. Hare went free because he gave evidence against his former partner in crime. He fled from Scotland to England for safety but died a penniless beggar on the streets of London.

4. Saving the bacon

Worried families often tried to safeguard their dead relatives against bodysnatchers. One way was to bury their loved one with strong steel hoops around the coffin. Another was to guard the graveyard every night – or pay someone else to guard it for them. This was not a pleasant job. One nervous guard armed himself with a pistol. When he saw a pale shape moving behind a tree he fired. When morning came he examined his victim . . . and found he had shot a pig!

5. Dead trouble

Perhaps the most ruthless bodysnatcher was Andrew

Merrilees. In 1818 his sister died. He had no hesitation in selling her corpse to the doctors!

Bodysnatching ended when a new law was passed in 1832 that granted doctors the right to experiment legally on bodies that came from a variety of sources. They therefore no longer needed to risk buying from bodysnatchers and the terrible business died out. However, the trade wasn't stopped simply because it shocked people. It was stopped because the gangs of bodysnatchers were causing too much trouble – it was not uncommon for two gangs to fight over a stolen body in the street!

7. "Don't go on the moors."

People have been telling stories about witches for thousands of years. There is even a witch in the Bible. Usually the stories are fantasies about eccentric old women flying around on broomsticks. The truth is less romantic. True tales of witchcraft often concern the helpless old victims of bullying mobs. But sometimes the victim would strike back . . .

The Yorkshire Dales, England – 1818

Don't go on the moors, my dears. The moor's a wild and lonely place. The moor's the place where you might meet with poor Auld Nan.

Who's that? Who's Nan? You've never heard of Nan? I'll tell you then, but don't blame me if she comes back and troubles you at night. Or if you dream about her in your bed.

Some say that Nan is old and grey – and some say she is a young, dark-haired lass. Others say that there are two of them out there. Old Nan and her young grand-daughter. Listen to the tale the men tell, then you can decide.

They say Auld Nan wears old dark clothes and lives out there alone amidst the bracken. No, no, no! She doesn't sleep out in the bracken, foolish child. She has a cottage out there – tumbled stone and wooden roof.

She begs for food, the sort of scraps that wouldn't keep a dog alive. The village folk all give her some . . . of course. They're too afraid of what will happen to them if they tell her no!

Ah, no, not all the folk are scared of poor Auld Nan. The men are not afraid – leastways they're not afraid so long as they are in a group. The sort of group that walked back home one night from Ilkley market. As they crossed the stream below the village they saw Nan. She sat up on the ridge and looked towards the sunset, doing no one any harm.

The evening breeze was lifting up her hair. It floated out behind her like a grey smoke from the orange setting sun. And something about her calmness drove the village men into a fury. "Auld Nan Hardwick . . . waiting for the devil to come along as soon as the sun sets!"

"Hag!" they called her. "Hag! Witch." The men threw stones. The stones all missed and that just made them angrier still. "The devil's wrapped her in his hand. We'll never hit her with a stone."

They drew together in a group and grumbled savagely to each other. "If she's a witch, she'll put a curse upon us now! Our wives and children won't be safe. We don't want her sort on our moor."

"What can we do?" a skinny ploughboy asked.

"We'll get the dogs to hound her out! We'll hunt her down just like a fox!" big Bart the tavern keeper hissed.

The men all clenched their fists in joy. They'd drive Auld Nan out and they'd have a good day's sport.

Next day they met in big Bart's inn with snarling, snapping dogs all straining at their leashes. Twenty of the ugliest brutes, all kept hungry while their owners drank a barrel of Bart's best beer. Then they set off through the autumn bracken till the hounds picked up her scent.

Soon they came in sight of Auld Nan's cottage. Nan was scratching at the stony soil to find a few thin carrots when the hunters slipped the leashes off the slavering dogs. They leapt forward while the woman lifted up her skirts and ran. She reached the battered wooden door a moment before the howling hounds. They crashed against it just as Nan threw in the bolt and stood there gasping for her breath.

The scrabbling, yowling furious pack seemed sure to claw their way clean through that door before the men came up and pulled the dogs off one by one. "Come out, Auld Nan!" the blacksmith called. "We won't harm you!"

"No we won't," big Bart hissed. "But our dogs will tear you flesh from bone."

"If you don't want to harm me, let me be," the woman called. Her voice was frail and quivering.

If the men felt pity then they didn't show it. The ploughboy pulled some bushes from the garden and he piled them up against the door. The cobbler from the village took a flint from out of his pocket and he started up a fire.

The bush was dry. It hadn't rained for weeks. It began to crackle as the crimson and gold flames took hold. Then the door began to smoulder, its ancient wood as dry as the dust on the daisies in Auld Nan's garden.

The woman screamed as the door burned through. The hunters and the hounds stepped back to keep from being roast alive. They saw the woman's figure, head down, burst out through the charcoal ruins of the door.

Her long legs carried her quickly though the bracken and she had a head start on the slobbering dogs. The men began to lumber through the thick brown fern and bay for blood just like their animals. The flying woman was fast as any hare. The men lost sight of her as she ran down into hollows then back across a ridge.

The dogs were tired and hungry. Weak for lack of food and losing interest. Then they heard a cry. "Leave me alone!" a woman screamed.

They turned. They looked back at the smoking ruin of Auld Nan's house. There she stood beside the door. The hunters lumbered back down the hill. The dogs' noses told them she was over the top of the hill. Their eyes told them she was running downhill from the house. They ran around in confusion then followed the men back down the hill.

The woman disappeared over the small bank that led to the stream. When the men reached it she was

86

not in sight. The dogs arrived at the water and sniffed along the edge. The scent disappeared into the water.

Just as big Bart began to say, "She must have run in a circle . . ." a voice came from the top of the ridge. "Leave me alone!"

The men looked up wide-mouthed and wondering at the figure in the flowing black skirts. "She didn't run!" the blacksmith howled. "She must have flown!"

The dogs were pleased to sight their victim again and began to lope up the hill while their owners tumbled after them. Of course, they reached the top . . . and saw the woman at the bottom.

The morning sun was burning hotter now and the men were thirsty and tired. They returned to the smoking cottage and kicked at Auld Nan's thin bedding and poor pots and pans. Then they went back to the village and drank another barrel of big Bart's beer and told themselves how brave they were to bully an old woman from her home.

All that autumn they boasted to their families that the village was safe from a fearsome witch. And so the village was. But the men who'd tormented the old woman were not.

Those men did not come home one winter night when they had been to Castleton Inn. The womenfolk went out at first light. Then they found the men below the bridge at Danby Dale. They slept, half frozen, on the river bed. If there had been more rain that year the river would have filled its banks and those drunken men would surely have drowned.

They told a weird tale. They said that during the night, as they had crossed the bridge, they saw Auld

Nan. Her shuffling, shambling, stumbling steps were taking her across the narrow bridge. The blacksmith blocked her way. The others stood behind him as he spoke. "There's only room for one to cross the bridge. Go back, you witch. Or fly across the stream!" he laughed. His friends behind him sniggered too.

And that's when Auld Nan raised her eyes up to the hills. A wind roared down and slapped the men like some huge icy hand. They clung on to the rail for as long as they could. It turned their blood to ice and when the wind died down they stood there like a row of statues. Auld Nan pushed her way across. They saw her pass but couldn't feel her withered body touch them on that narrow bridge.

They said they'd lost all sense, then fell into the icy trickling stream.

Now, some have said the men were drunk. They said they'd fallen off that bridge themselves. The story of Auld Nan's revenge was just a tavern tale they'd dreamed up in their fuddled brains.

And yet it's true that Nan was seen again next spring. Smoke was curling from her cottage chimney and two young farmers told a tale of their adventure on the moor.

It seems they'd met a girl out gathering flowers and they had called, "It's getting dark. The moors are no place for a lady at night!"

She moved away when they came close. They reached to grab her but she slipped from their grasp like some young bird and ran across the heather.

The farmers decided to set out after her. She ran fast but they were young and fit and kept her in their view. "You'll get nowhere!" one cried. "There are no places on the moor for you to hide."

She didn't stop but rushed across the darkening, grey-green moor until she reached the cottage of Auld Nan.

The farmers knew they'd caught their quarry inside the old stone-walled cottage. They marched up to the door and rattled at the latch. They called "Come out, my pretty!"

Then they heard the bolts slide back and from the shadowy crack the face of Auld Nan peered out at them. "Evening, sirs," she smiled. "How nice to have some company in my lonely house. Come in and share a glass of heather wine with me. It's rare that I have visitors here. So, tell me, what brings you gents out to see old Nan?"

"A dark-haired girl," one said. "She'd lost her way upon the moors. We thought we'd see her safe back home. Perhaps she called in here to ask the way?" His partner looked around the gloomy room, the only light the amber glow from Nan's peat fire.

"A dark-haired girl, you say? There's no girl here! I'll stir the fire and give you light so you can look round for yourself," the woman said, and threw a dry branch on the fire.

In the flickering yellow flame the men looked round the room. The woman's tumbled bedding lay in the corner. No girl there. Two stools stood beside the fire and Nan said, "Sit down, gentlemen, and warm yourselves."

The farmers sat before the fire and Auld Nan added still more logs. "They say if you look in the flames you see your future in the pictures there. So, look, my friends!" she said as the young men sat down. She leaned back in her rocking chair and then she threw more logs upon the fire.

The men looked in the fire and something in there held their gaze. The pictures enchanted them until they could not move and still the fire grew brighter and hotter. "Watch the flames, just watch the flames," the woman chuckled as the heat began to singe their eyebrows, then their hair.

Then their clothes began to smoulder and their faces felt the fire's fierce scorch. Still the farmers had no power to move and Auld Nan's laughter became a wild shriek. "Can you see your wild girl, young men? Can you see her in the flames?"

Then at last she broke the spell and let the farmers fall away from those fiendish flames. They raised their hands to blistered faces, sobbed and stumbled to the door. Feeling the cool evening air, they staggered down the horse trail to their village.

"Come and visit any time!" the woman called and cackled. "Any time you're passing by. If I see your dark-haired maiden I'll be sure to send your love!" she screeched as harsh as any curlew calling from the moor.

The village people never bothered Nan again. Can you blame them?

So don't go on the moors, my dears. The moor's a wild and lonely place. But, if you do, and if you meet her, treat her kindly. After all, she's just a woman like your old Gran, isn't she?

Witches — FACT FILE

This story was recorded in a 16th-century book on witchcraft. For thousands of years people have picked out the weakest among them to bully and torment. If the victims were harmless, the bullies invented a reason to harm them. If the victim was a lonely woman, for example, then she was often accused of 'Witchcraft'.

1. Selling the soul
A witch was said to have made a deal with the Devil – she gave the Devil her soul, for which he gave her magical powers. A witch could be a woman or a man, but was more often a woman.

2. Familiar friend
The devil was said to send a 'familiar' to help a witch. This was often a cat, a toad or a dog.

3. No way to win
The punishment for witchcraft in England and America was hanging. In Scotland and in Europe they were burned. Witches were often tortured until they confessed to dealing with the devil. Once they had confessed they were executed. If they didn't confess, then they could be set a form of trial. 'Ducking' was a popular witch-trial. This entailed the victim being tied hand and foot and thrown into a river or pond. If she floated then the accusers said the devil was helping her. They took her out and executed her. If she sank

then she was innocent – but of course she could well have drowned. Either way she died.

4. Cruel mistakes
A simple trial was to ask a suspect to recite the Lord's Prayer without making a mistake. Knowing that a slight slip could cost your life is enough to make anyone nervous enough to make a dozen mistakes. There were times when witch-hunting became a 'mania' in certain countries. Dozens of witches were accused, who in turn tried to save their lives by accusing others. The accusers and the accused were all executed after very unfair trials.

5. Unfair trials and tribulations
In Stuart England a 'witch-finder' was often appointed. He was paid every time he discovered a witch – the more he found the more money he made. So, of course, he planned an unfair test to prove a victim was a witch. He looked for the mark of the devil on the skin – any birth mark or mole would do. He said that a normal human would bleed if this mark was pricked – a witch would not bleed. He then appeared to stick a pin into the mark. If it didn't bleed then the victim was hanged. But it was a fraud. The pin-prick didn't bleed because it was a fake needle. Eventually, witch-finders were unmasked as frauds. Many were hanged.

6. Sad prayer
In the 16th century a prayer was written which shows that not everyone was as stupidly superstitious as the

others . . .

For all those who died – stripped naked, shaved, shorn.
For those who screamed in vain to God, only to have their tongues ripped out by the root.
For those who were pricked, racked, broken on the wheel for the sins of the witch-hunters.
For those whose beauty stirred their torturers to fury.
For those whose ugliness did the same.
For those who were neither ugly nor beautiful, but only women who would not confess.
For those quick fingers broken in the vice.
For those soft arms pulled from their sockets.
For all those witch-women, my sisters, who breathed freer as the flames took them, knowing as they shed their female bodies, that death would shed them of the sin for which they died – the sin of being born a woman.